Seasons of Endearment

written and illustrated by
Emily Williams-Wheeler

Adventure Publications
Cambridge, Minnesota

Copyright ©1993 by Emily Williams Wheeler

Published by
Adventure Publications, Inc.
P.O. Box 269
Cambridge, MN 55008

All rights reserved
Printed in the United States of America
ISBN 0-934860-06-8

For you.

It begins

as a diamond in the rough.

Then come fragrant offerings,

a sweet rendez-vous,

and wishing on the same star.

There are endless days
that float along

and an awkward giggle or two.

Two moving together as one

to the moment
we've been waiting for.

It begins again, a renaissance,

a world filled up by two,

then, wonderfully, three.

Precious moments, precious firsts.

We savor three together,

but still find time for two.

We capture highlights

and gather memories

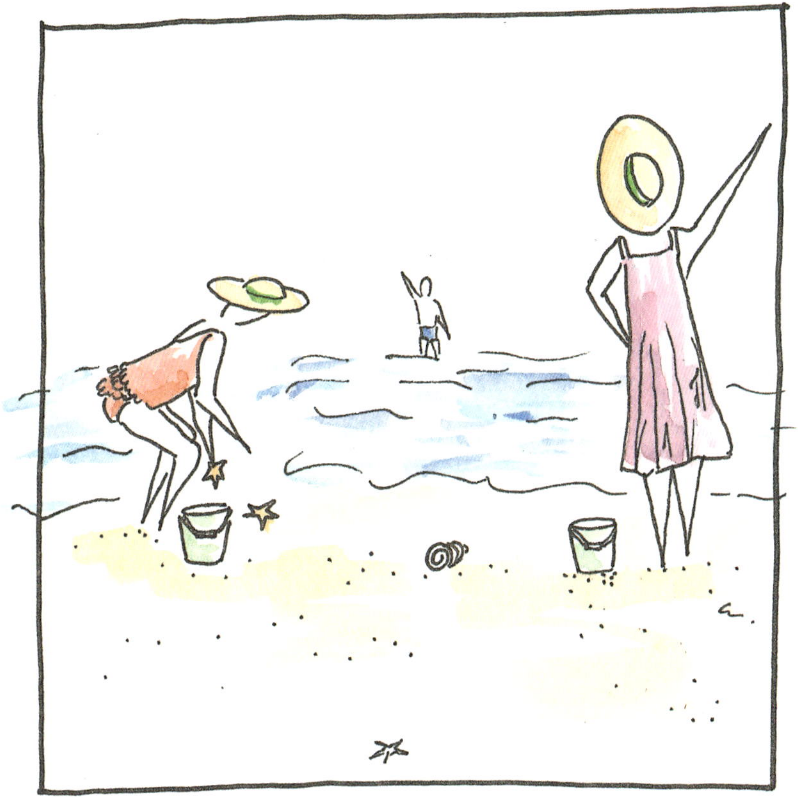

until the nest empties

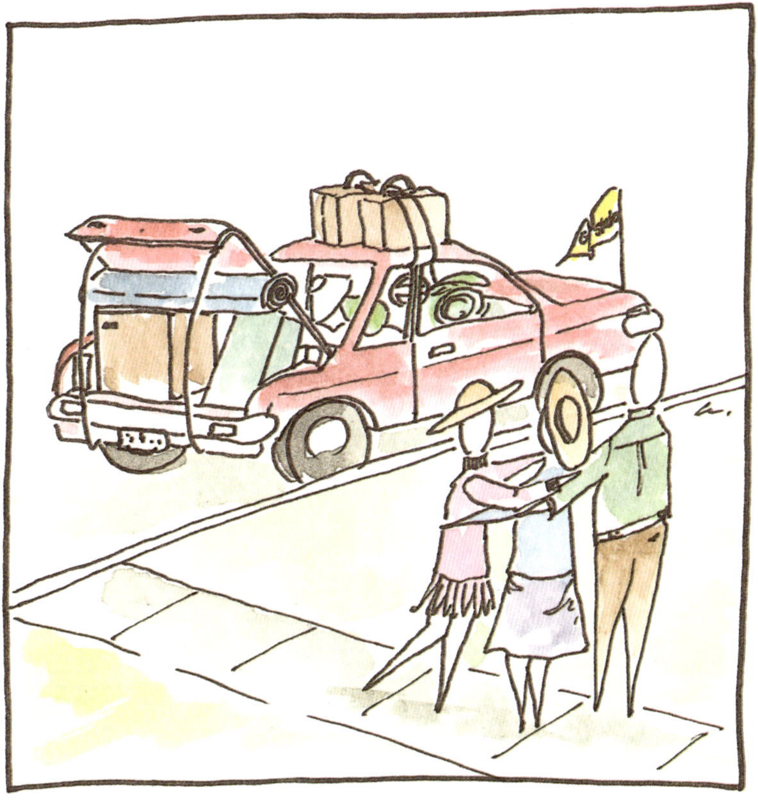

and other nests are made.

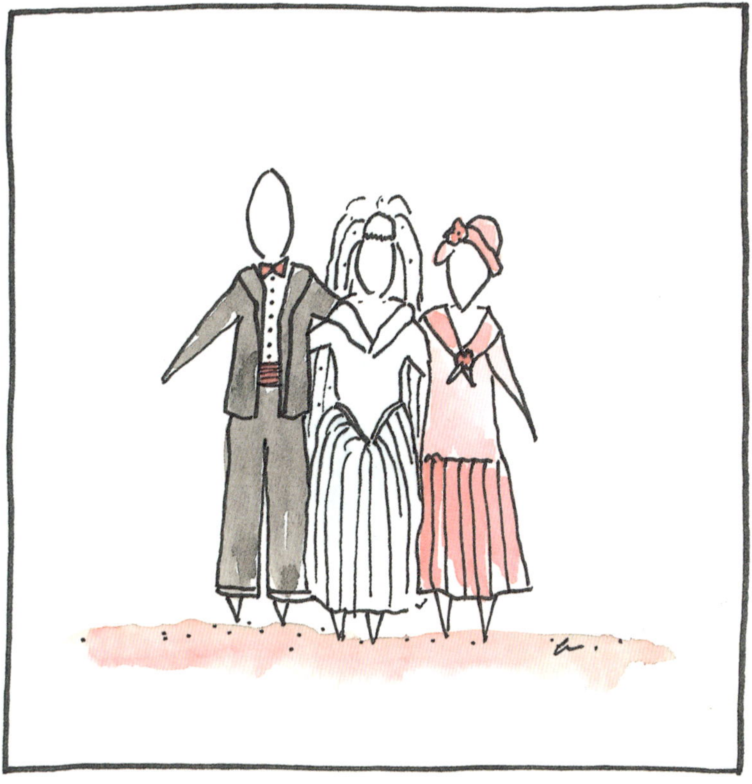

Home alone!

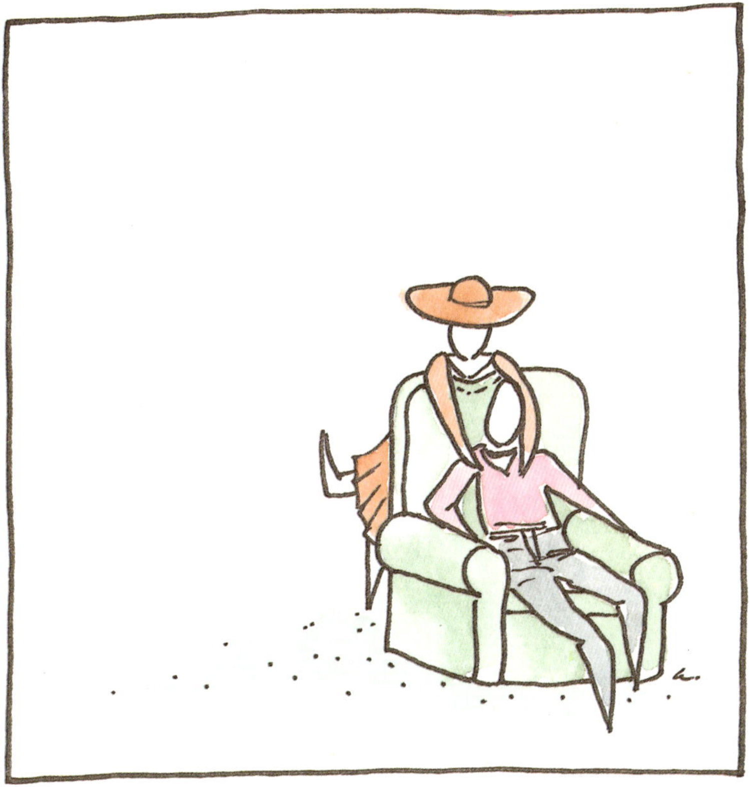

for a moonlight serenade.

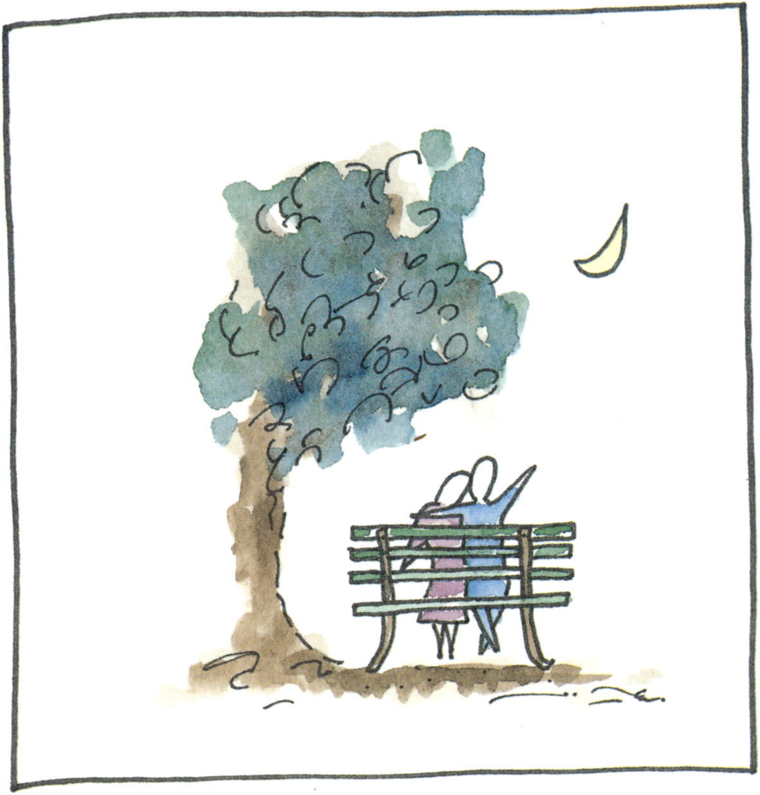

The road goes on,

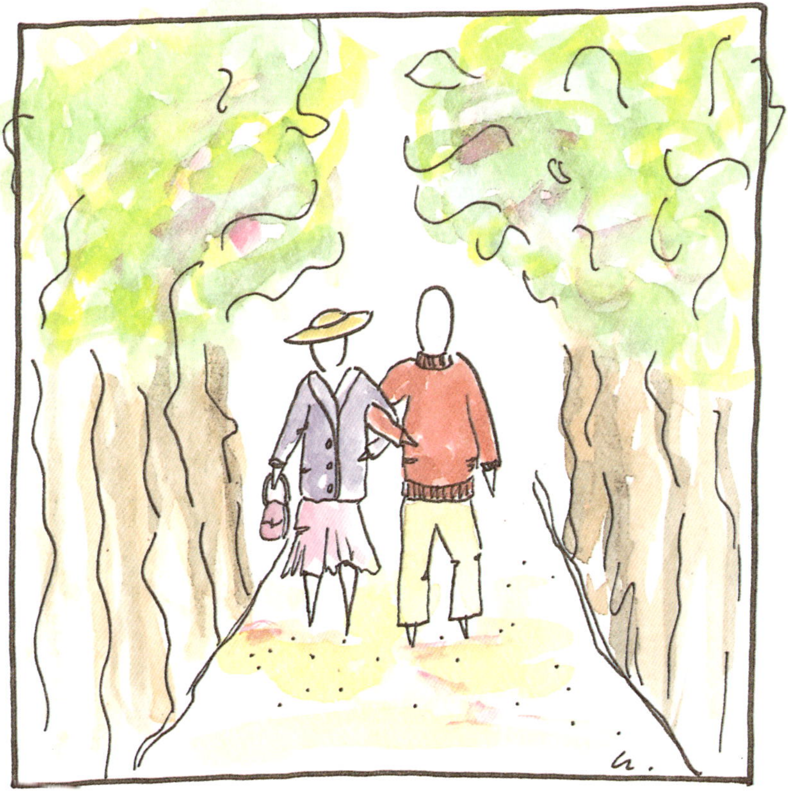

the cycle of love continues,

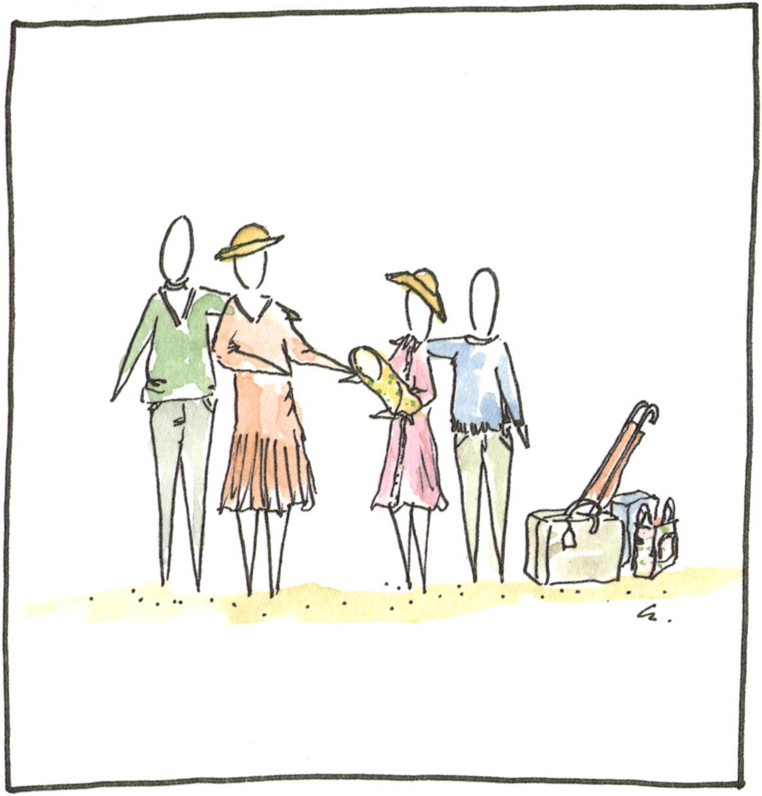

as the embers still burn brightly

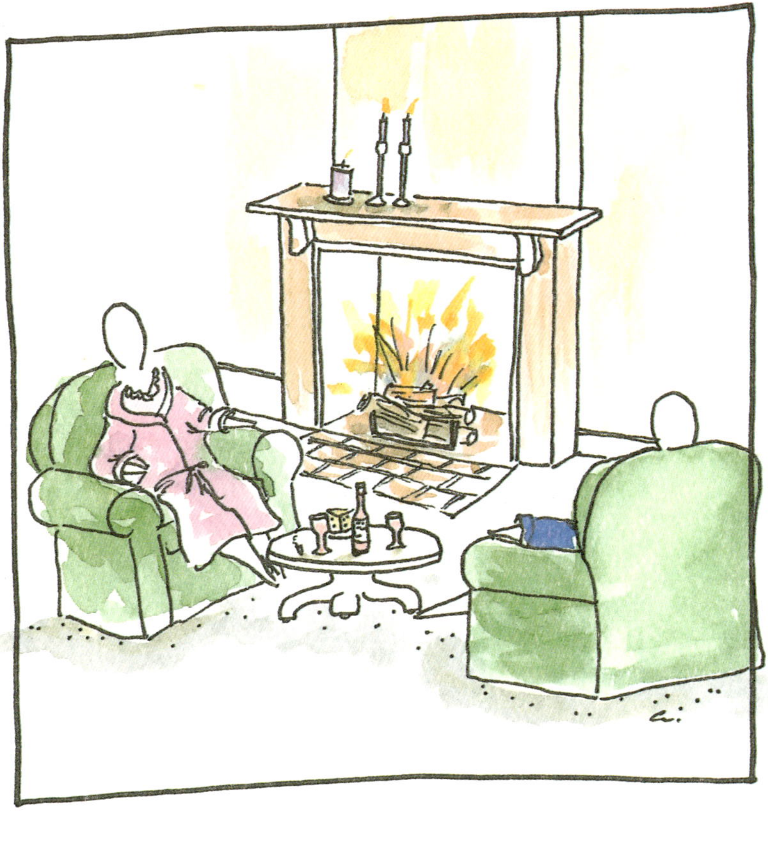

for you, the night, and the music.

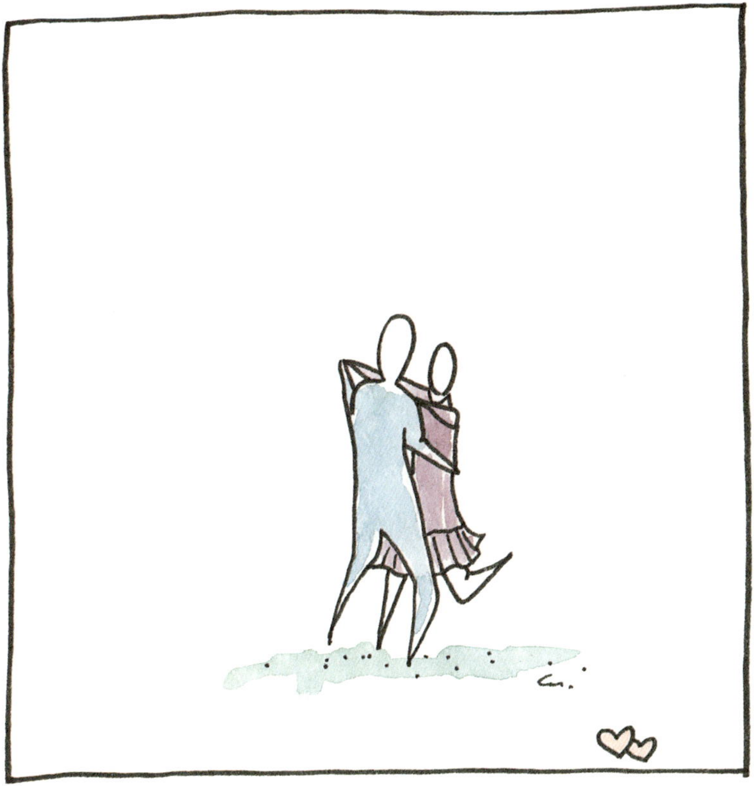

For more information on books and jewelry by Emily Williams-Wheeler, contact your local gift/book store or Adventure Publications 1·800·678·7006.